The painting was gone!

"There's a note!" exclaimed Sarah-Jane.

The note was scribbled on the back of that day's church bulletin.

"Did someone from the church take the painting?" Aunt Sarah asked. "How strange to leave a present—and then come and take it back."

Titus said, "Maybe someone from the church took the painting, but it wasn't the artist. Look!"

It's time for the T.C.D.C. to get to work!

THE MYSTERY OF THE

VANISHING PRESENT

Elspeth Campbell Murphy
Illustrated by Chris Wold Dyrud

Chariot Books
David C. Cook Publishing Co.

A Wise Owl Book
Published by Chariot Books,
an imprint of David C. Cook Publishing Co.
David C. Cook Publishing Co., Elgin, Illinois 60120
David C. Cook Publishing Co., Weston, Ontario

The Mystery of the Vanishing Present
Cover design by Chris Patchel
First Printing, 1988
Printed in the United States of America
93 92   10 9 8 7 6

Library of Congress Cataloging-in-Publication Data
Murphy, Elspeth Campbell.
    The mystery of the vanishing present.

    (The Ten Commandments mysteries)
    Summary: Three cousins endeavor to find out who gave a
painting entitled "Sabbath Day" to their grandfather for a birthday
present.
    [1. Cousins—Fiction. 2. Ten commandments—Sabbath—
Fiction. 3. Mystery and detective stories]
I. Dyrud, Chris Wold, ill. II. Title. III. Series:
Murphy, Elspeth Campbell. Ten Commandments mysteries.
PZ7.M95316My   1988   [FIC]   87-20852
ISBN 1-55513-364-9

''Remember the Sabbath day by keeping it holy.''

Exodus 20:8 (NIV)

CONTENTS

1
LEONARDO

It was Sunday morning, and Timothy Dawson woke up bright and early—as usual.

From the moment he opened his eyes, Timothy was always full of energy, wanting to be up and doing stuff.

He looked across the little room in his grandparents' house, to where his cousin Titus McKay was curled up in a sleeping bag.

"Hey, Ti!" Timothy called softly. "Are you awake?"

But Timothy knew it was no use. It would take a stick of dynamite to wake Titus up this early in the morning.

Timothy crawled out of his own sleeping bag and put on his bathrobe and slippers. Then he tiptoed across the hallway to his grandmother's sewing room and peeked inside.

Timothy's other cousin, Sarah-Jane Cooper, was curled up sound asleep on a rollaway bed.

And nearby, in her crib, Timothy's little sister, Priscilla, was making funny little baby noises in her sleep.

The night before, Sarah-Jane had begged and begged until the grown-ups finally said Priscilla could sleep in the sewing room with her.

Timothy thought to himself, "S-J acts like Priscilla is a baby doll who came to life. Well, *I* don't see what's so great about having Priscilla around. All she does is sleep and cry and make all kinds of messes."

Timothy turned away from the door and went downstairs.

There were lots of relatives in his grandparents' house this weekend. Timothy counted them on his fingers.

First there was his mother, Sarah, and his father, Paul.

Then there were his mother's parents—Grandma and Grandpa Gordon, who lived there. Grandpa was the pastor of the church next door.

Then there was his mother's sister, Aunt Jane, and her husband, Uncle Richard—and their son, Titus.

Then there was his mother's other sister, Aunt Sue, and her husband, Uncle Art—and their daughter, Sarah-Jane. (Sarah-Jane was named after both her aunts.)

Timothy frowned thoughtfully. Who was he forgetting? Oh, yes—Priscilla. And himself, of course. That made twelve people in all.

Two parents. Two grandparents. Two aunts. Two uncles. Two cousins. And one baby sister.

It was lonely being the only wide-awake one in a house full of eleven sleeping people.

But Timothy's parents had this rule: Whenever Timothy got up super early, he could fix himself some cereal and find something quiet to do. But he couldn't go around waking everybody else up.

Grandma always bought the kids' favorite cereals for them. Timothy fixed himself a bowl and carried it out onto the front porch.

Suddenly he was not alone anymore.

A frisky little dog came bouncing across the porch, grinning and wagging his tail.

"Hello, boy!" Timothy cried. "You're a good dog, aren't you? A good, good dog!"

The little dog planted his front paws on Timothy's lap as if to say, "I couldn't agree with you more!"

Timothy hoped the dog was a stray and that his parents would say he could keep him. He didn't *really* think that would happen, but you never could tell. . . .

But the little dog *wasn't* a stray. He was wearing a dog tag that said *Leonardo*.

"That's a funny name for a dog," Timothy

thought.

Just then there came a whistle from behind the bushes by the front sidewalk. Timothy couldn't see who it was. But he thought the whistler sounded nervous—maybe about the dog being on someone else's porch.

Leonardo *was* a good little dog. He obeyed the whistle right away.

And Timothy found himself alone once more.

He was just turning to go back inside the house, when he saw the mysterious package.

2
THE PACKAGE

When Timothy saw the package, he thought of the words to a song: *Brown paper packages tied up with string, these are a few of my favorite things.*

The package was in the shape of a rectangle. It was about the size of a place mat. But it was much heavier than that.

Of course, Timothy was dying to open the package. He didn't see a card anywhere to tell who the package was from or who it was for.

"Who knows?" he said to himself. "Maybe it's for *me*!"

But he didn't *really* believe that. After all, the package was left on his grandparents' porch. And tomorrow—the Fourth of July—was his grandfather's birthday.

His grandfather always said that he was born on the same day the Declaration of Independence was signed.

When Timothy, Titus, and Sarah-Jane were little, they used to think their grandfather was serious.

But when they got older, they figured out that he would have to be 'way over two hundred years old. *Nobody* was *that* old!

And Grandpa always claimed that the fireworks were in honor of his birthday! Timothy, Titus, and Sarah-Jane used to believe that, too. But nowadays they just groaned whenever he said that.

Still, it was nice that Grandpa had a birthday on a holiday. Every summer the whole family got together to celebrate.

Timothy carried the mysterious package inside. He decided that this was worth waking the family up for. He decided to start with Sarah-Jane.

But when he got to the sewing room, he saw that Sarah-Jane was already awake.

She was standing by Priscilla's crib.

Sarah-Jane had been given strict orders not to

15

get Priscilla up to play. So Sarah-Jane wasn't poking Priscilla or shaking her. Instead, she was just looking at the baby really hard, trying to make her wake up on her own.

Timothy said, "S-J, if you want to wake somebody up, come help me with Titus."

"Okay, I'll help," said Sarah-Jane. "Got any dynamite?"

It took a long time and a lot of work. But Sarah-Jane and Timothy finally got Titus out of his sleeping bag.

Timothy explained about the package.

His cousins agreed that it was definitely mysterious! And all three of them *loved* mysteries!

Sarah-Jane asked, "You're sure there was no card or note or *anything*?"

Timothy shrugged. "I looked all around, and I didn't see anything."

Titus said, "Hey, wait a minute. There *is* a note. It's printed right on the brown wrapping paper."

Timothy and Sarah-Jane looked up close at the spot where Titus was pointing.

They saw little teeny-tiny letters that said, *Happy Birthday, Pastor Gordon!*

"So I was right," said Timothy. "The package is for Grandpa."

"That printing is so neat and tiny!" said Sarah-Jane.

"Yes," said Titus. "And it wasn't made with a

pencil or a pen. It looks like it was *painted* on."

"Who could paint something that little?" asked Sarah-Jane.

"And who would just leave a present on somebody's front porch like that?" asked Titus.

"But most of all," said Timothy, "WHAT'S IN THE PACKAGE?"

They were just about to knock on their grandparents' bedroom door, when Priscilla yelled her little baby head off. And that woke *everyone* up.

"It's not fair," Timothy said to Titus and Sarah-Jane. "I have to be *so quiet*, and she gets to make all the noise she wants.

"MOM! Cilly's crying!"

"So I hear!" said Timothy's mother, shuffling into the sewing room. "And, Timothy, please don't call your baby sister Silly."

Timothy said, "I wasn't calling her Silly with an S. I was calling her Cilly with a C."

"Well, just call her Priscilla," said his mother with a yawn. "What's that package you're holding?"

"It's for Grandpa, Aunt Sarah!" cried Sarah-Jane excitedly.

18

"Yes, Aunt Sarah," said Titus. "Someone just left it on the front porch, and Tim just found it."

"A package for me?" said Grandpa, joining them. "Well, let's not wait another minute!"

He tore off the brown paper wrapping, and the whole family gathered around to see what was inside the mysterious package.

It was a *painting*—a beautiful little painting.

It was done all in bright colors. And it showed a pretty, little white church. Lots of people were coming out of the church. They were gathering in groups on the lawn, laughing and talking.

There was so much *detail* you could hardly take it all in.

The title on the frame said SABBATH DAY.

"Oh, it's lovely!" breathed Grandma. "It just *looks* like a Sunday, doesn't it? The whole mood of the picture is so happy and peaceful. People are worshiping God and enjoying being together."

Suddenly Timothy said, "Grandma! Grandpa! That's *your* church in the painting!"

"Why, my goodness, Timothy!" cried

Grandpa. "You're right! So it is. I didn't realize it at first. But then I didn't *expect* to see my own church in a painting."

"And Grandpa!" cried Sarah-Jane. "There's *you*! You're standing at the door of the church, shaking hands with people."

Everyone crowded around to get a closer look.

And everyone agreed that it certainly was Grandpa in the painting.

"And look!" said Titus. "There's *me*!"

His mother said, "Sweetheart, why would you be in this picture? It's Grandpa's church, not our church in the city."

"But it *is* me!" insisted Titus. "See the boy with the broken arm? That's *me* when I had *my* broken arm. I'm talking to Tim and S-J. Look!"

"We're in the picture, too?" cried Timothy and Sarah-Jane together. "Let's see! Let's see!"

And, sure enough, they were.

5
MAGGIE

And then they found Grandma. And Aunt Sarah and Uncle Paul. And Aunt Jane and Uncle Richard. And Aunt Sue and Uncle Art.

"We're *all* in it!" said Grandma. "Plus all these people from the church. This is amazing artwork! The figures are so small. Yet you can easily tell who's who."

"When was this picture taken?" asked Timothy. "I mean, I know it wasn't 'taken' like a photograph. But why does it show us all together at Grandma and Grandpa's?"

Uncle Richard said, "It must have been when we were all here the last Fourth of July. That's when Titus had a broken arm, right, son?"

"Right," said Titus.

Sarah-Jane said, "Aunt Sarah, where's little

Priscilla in this picture?''

"She wasn't born yet," said Timothy's mother with a smile.

"Oh, yeah!" said Sarah-Jane, laughing at herself. Then she turned to nuzzle Priscilla. "You weren't born yet, were you? You sweet, sweet, *sweet* little baby!"

Priscilla laughed and cooed.

"Give me a break," thought Timothy. But out loud he said, "Grandpa, who painted this picture? It's probably someone who goes to your church, right?"

Grandpa turned to Grandma with a puzzled frown. "We don't know anyone who paints, do we, dear? But the artist does certainly seem to know us and our family."

Grandma said, "We were so busy finding ourselves in the picture that we forgot to look for a signature."

Uncle Art said, "Painters often sign their work in the lower right-hand corner."

And, sure enough, in little, teeny-tiny letters there was the name *Maggie*. No last name. Just *Maggie*.

Timothy said, "Guess what. The printing on the picture is the same kind of tiny printing that's on the wrapping paper. It's easy to figure out what happened. A friend of Grandma and Grandpa—named Maggie—painted this picture. Then she wrapped it up and left it out on the front porch for you—as a birthday present. Case closed! Mystery solved!"

But Grandma and Grandpa just shook their heads, looking more puzzled than ever. "We don't know anyone called Maggie," they said.

6
THE DRAGON

It was a mystery all right. And Timothy, Titus, and Sarah-Jane were just itching to solve it.

But there were eight grown-ups and four kids (counting Priscilla) who all had to get ready for church—at the same time. So the house got a little crazy for a while.

After breakfast (Timothy's second), the three cousins wandered out onto the screened-in back porch.

Grandpa liked to sit out there and go over his sermon before walking across to church.

But he wasn't reading his sermon now. He had brought the painting out onto the back porch with him. And he was studying it carefully.

Grandpa looked up at Timothy, Titus, and Sarah-Jane with a smile and said, "The more you look, the more you see."

"Who's that lady?" asked Titus, pointing to a frowning figure in the picture. "She sure doesn't look very happy and peaceful!"

Grandpa sighed. "That's Mrs. Drayton. I'm afraid she's one of those people who complains about *everything*—the sermon, the hymns, even the flowers!"

"She looks very bossy," said Sarah-Jane. "You can tell just by the way she's standing."

Just then Grandma joined them. She said, "Mrs. Drayton means well, I suppose. But she always wants to have things her own way. She always thinks she knows what's best for everybody else."

Titus said, "It sounds like Mrs. Drayton should really be called Mrs. *Dragon*!"

Grandma and Grandpa looked at each other and burst out laughing. "The things your grandchildren come out with!" exclaimed Grandpa, pretending to be shocked.

Grandma asked, "Is Margaret in the picture, too? Oh, yes. I see her."

Then she explained, "Margaret is Mrs. Dray-

ton's niece. She lives with her aunt. Poor Margaret. She's a very nice young woman. But she's *so* shy and timid. Almost like a little mouse.''

Timothy said, ''The Dragon and the Mouse.''

Grandpa chuckled and said, ''Exactly!''

And just then—the Dragon herself came charging across the church lawn toward the house.

''Mrs. Gordon! I want a word with you!'' Mrs. Drayton demanded.

Grandma held open the screen door for her. Mrs. Drayton stomped into the porch and said, ''Whoever is in charge of making the coffee bought the WRONG KIND! I never—''

She stopped suddenly and stared open mouthed, at the SABBATH DAY painting. ''Where did you get that?'' she snapped.

''It was given to me as a birthday present,'' said Grandpa nicely but firmly.

''Yes, isn't it lovely?'' said Grandma.

''Humph!'' snorted the Dragon. ''I'm sure I don't know.''

''Now, what were you saying about the coffee?'' asked Grandma.

But to their great surprise, Mrs. Drayton turned and hurried away.

They all stood staring after her for a moment.

But then Sarah-Jane and Titus had to go finish getting ready.

And Grandma and Grandpa went across the yard to church early.

So Timothy was left alone on the porch with SABBATH DAY.

Grandpa was right about the painting. The more you looked, the more you saw.

Suddenly Timothy sat up straight and stared. Here was something that he hadn't noticed before—a frisky little dog! In the picture, the dog was bounding across the yard as if he had been waiting for someone to come out of church. Timothy could hardly believe his eyes. He was sure the dog in the painting was Leonardo, the same little dog he had seen earlier that morning.

7
LEONARDO AGAIN

In all the hustle and bustle of getting over to church, Timothy managed to ask his father something. "Dad, what kind of name is *Leonardo*?"

Timothy's father was busy chasing Priscilla's sun hat, which she had thrown on the ground. So he didn't have time to wonder why Timothy was asking such a strange question.

"It's an Italian name," he said. "There was a famous painter named Leonardo. Leonardo da Vinci."

"Hmmm," said Timothy. He walked off slowly by himself. He was thinking very hard.

Sarah-Jane and Titus caught up to him.

"What's up, Tim?" asked Sarah-Jane.

"Yeah, Tim," said Titus. "You have a funny look on your face."

Timothy said, "I think I just figured something out. . . . This morning I saw this neat-O little dog on the front porch. The name on his tag said *Leonardo*."

Titus said, "Who would name a dog *Leonardo*?"

"That's just it, Ti," said Timothy. "Leonardo was a famous artist. So someone who likes to *paint* might name a dog Leonardo. And that's not all. The dog was on the front porch just before I found the *present*. I think he came along when the *artist* dropped the painting off."

Titus said thoughtfully, "So Leonardo is Maggie's dog."

Sarah-Jane sighed. "Yes, but we still don't know who Maggie is."

"But I think I know a way to find out," said Timothy.

"How?" cried Titus and Sarah-Jane together.

Timothy said, "That's what I figured out! See, Leonardo is in the SABBATH DAY painting! In the picture, he was running across the yard toward the people. If we can look at the painting and tell *who he's running to*, we'll know who his owner is!''

Sarah-Jane's eyes were shining with excitement. ''And then we'll know who painted the picture! Because Leonardo's owner is the artist—Mysterious Maggie!''

''This is so EXcellent!'' said Titus. ''Right after church, we'll look at the painting and identify the artist.''

But after church, when the detective cousins burst into the back porch, they discovered that the SABBATH DAY painting was gone.

8

A JOB FOR THE T.C.D.C.

"Oh, no!" cried Grandpa. "Why didn't I take the time to put the painting away inside the house?"

"Don't blame yourself, Dad," said Aunt Sue. "It never occurred to any of us that the painting wouldn't be safe on the back porch. And it's odd that the burglar didn't take anything else. . . ."

"Mom!" interrupted Sarah-Jane. "There's a *note*! It must have blown on the floor." Sarah-Jane stooped and picked it up.

The note was scribbled on the back of that day's church bulletin. In big, scrawly letters it said: *Pastor Gordon, I'm sorry to have to do this. But it's for the best.*

Aunt Sarah said, "Why is it written on the bulletin? Does that mean someone *from the church* took the painting?''

Aunt Jane said, ''Was it the artist? How strange to leave a present—and then come and take it back!''

Titus said, ''Maybe someone from church took the painting away. But it wasn't the artist. See? The printing is different! The printing on the note is big. The printing on the wrapping is tiny. The artist *left* the painting early this morning. But *somebody else* took it away while we were in church.''

They were all saying how smart that was of Titus, when a timid little voice said, ''Uh, excuse me.''

They all turned to see a shy-looking young woman standing on the porch steps.

''Why, Margaret! Come in,'' said Grandma warmly. She opened the door wide and gently pulled Margaret onto the porch. Grandma added, ''We were all just about to go out for lunch. Won't you join us?''

''Oh!—uh—thank you!—But I can't. My— my aunt will be waiting for me. I just came over to return the baby's sun hat. I think she threw it

on the nursery floor." Margaret swallowed hard. "What's all the commotion here?"

Grandpa said, "It seems I have a vanishing present!" And he explained everything that had been going on with the painting. Then he said, "This is a job for the T.C.D.C."

"What's a 'teesy-deesy'?" asked Margaret.

"It's letters," explained Timothy.

"Capital T.

Capital C.

Capital D.

Capital C.

It stands for the Three Cousins Detective Club.''

Margaret nodded shyly and scurried away.

"Well," said Timothy to his detective cousins. "First we had to figure out where Grandpa's painting *came from*. Now we have to figure out where it *went*."

Grandpa agreed that they would have to get to the bottom of things. But he said, "It's always so busy when we're all here. And this disappearing present has made things even busier! I think we need to take a few minutes to be quiet and thankful before we rush off to lunch."

So the whole family sat in a big circle in the living room. And each person told one thing he or she was thankful for. (Priscilla just gurgled, of course. But Sarah-Jane claimed Priscilla was thankful for the fuss people made over her in the nursery.)

Grandma was the last one. She said, "I have *two* things. First, I'm thankful that someone cared enough about us to give us that beautiful painting. And second, I'm thankful we have the T.C.D.C. to help us find out where it went!"

Timothy, Titus, and Sarah-Jane felt all warm

and happy when she said that. And they were more determined than ever to get to the bottom of things. They would begin looking for the painting right after lunch.

But when the family returned from lunch, the painting was back.

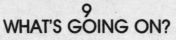

Propped up against the painting was a note. In tiny, neat letters it said, *Pastor and Mrs. Gordon, I really want you to have this*.

"What in the world is going on?" asked Grandma.

Timothy, Titus, and Sarah-Jane knew that the little, tiny letters on the note must have been written by Maggie. That meant Maggie was the one who brought the painting back. And they knew how to find out who Maggie was.

They rushed to the painting to see who Leonardo was running to.

He was running straight to Margaret Drayton.

"Margaret!?" cried Grandma, when the cousins explained about Leonardo belonging to the artist. "*Margaret* painted SABBATH DAY?

Why, of course! *Maggie* is short for *Margaret.*"

Grandpa said, "Her aunt always calls her Margaret. But—who knows? Maybe she wants to be known as Maggie. I think we'd better give Margaret—I mean, Maggie—a call and see what's going on."

Grandpa came back from the phone and said, "Margaret—I mean, Maggie—said that the T.C.D.C. was pretty smart to have figured out who painted the picture and left it for me. But she also said there's a lot we don't understand. She wants to explain everything. So she's invited us over."

"*All* of us?" asked Timothy's mother.

"Yes," said Grandpa. "She said she wants to show us something."

So they all went out for a Sunday afternoon walk over to Mrs. Drayton's house.

Grandpa took the painting with him. "I don't want my present to disappear again!" he said.

Sarah-Jane pushed Priscilla in her stroller, cooing to her the whole time.

"Give me a break!" thought Timothy. But out loud he said, "There's Maggie and Leonardo!

They came out to meet us.''

Leonardo rushed up to Timothy and greeted him like a long-lost friend. Timothy introduced the little dog to Titus and Sarah-Jane.

Then Sarah-Jane introduced Leonardo to Priscilla. "See the nice doggy-woggy?" she asked.

Timothy and Titus looked at each other and rolled their eyes and groaned.

"All right, all right," Sarah-Jane said to the boys. "See the nice DOG, Priscilla?"

Maggie led them to the room over the garage. It was a big room, filled with light. And everywhere there were paintings—beautiful, brightly colored paintings.

Maggie looked both shy and proud at the same time. "My studio," she said softly.

"Oh, Maggie! These are *wonderful!*" the grown-ups all exclaimed.

"Neat-O!" said Timothy.

"EXcellent!" said Titus.

"See the pretty, pretty pictures, Priscilla?" asked Sarah-Jane.

Maggie blushed pink with pleasure.

But suddenly a harsh voice from the doorway said, "And *what*, may I ask, is going on up here?"

SABBATH DAY

Everyone jumped.

"The Dragon!" whispered Timothy to Titus and Sarah-Jane.

Maggie glanced at her aunt. Then she cleared her throat and turned to Grandpa. "Pastor Gordon, your grandchildren figured out that *I* was the one who left the SABBATH DAY painting on your front porch this morning. I know that probably wasn't the best way to give it to you. But—well—I didn't know if you'd like it—and—and—"

"And *I* was the one who took it back again!" declared Mrs. Drayton grandly.

"But, *why*?" asked Grandma, as if she could hardly believe her ears.

"Because it's part of a *set*!" said Mrs. Drayton

firmly.

Everyone looked at Maggie. "Uh, yes—yes, it is," said Maggie. "It's from my Days-of-the-Week series." She pointed to a row of six pictures propped against the wall.

Each picture was filled with people busily working and playing. And each picture showed a different scene from Grandma's and Grandpa's town. The paintings were delightful.

Mrs. Drayton said, "A friend of Margaret's showed the paintings to an art dealer. And the dealer wants to display the Days-of-the-Week series in his gallery. The set is *not complete* without SABBATH DAY!"

Maggie said to her aunt, "But I really wanted Pastor and Mrs. Gordon to have this painting! They help to make Sundays so special for all of us. And I wanted to do something to thank them. I don't want SABBATH DAY to be sold to somebody else!"

Maggie turned back to Grandma and Grandpa. "When I came over with the baby's sun hat, I found out that someone took your painting. And I knew right away who that was!"

Maggie looked right at her aunt.

"Humph!" snorted the Dragon. "I did what had to be done!"

Maggie looked back to the Gordons. "I was so embarrassed! So, while you were all gone to lunch, I brought the painting back!"

Grandpa placed his painting beside the other six. " 'Remember the Sabbath Day by keeping it holy,' " he said. "That's Number Four of the Ten Commandments. We have six days to do all our work—as these pictures show. But God understands what people are like. He knows we need time out to rest and think about life's most important things. The week wouldn't be complete without Sunday."

He smiled gently at Maggie. "And your Days-of-the-Week series wouldn't be complete without SABBATH DAY, Maggie. You can't imagine how much Mrs. Gordon and I love this painting! It's very hard for us to think of giving it up. But I don't want to spoil your display at the gallery. Perhaps someone will want to buy all seven."

Maggie looked delighted at the idea that some-

one might buy the whole series. But she looked
sad at the idea of taking back SABBATH DAY
from Grandma and Grandpa.

Suddenly she said, "I know! I'll paint you a
new SABBATH DAY!"

Timothy could tell that his grandparents *really
liked* that idea. But they were too polite to agree
to let Maggie go to all that work.

Then Timothy thought of something important
that would help them say "Yes."

He spoke up loud and clear. "We really need a
new SABBATH DAY. You know why? Because

Priscilla isn't in the old one. She wasn't even born yet. But now she's in our family. So we should have her in the picture, too."

Maggie laughed happily. "Then it's settled!"

"Settled!" said Grandma and Grandpa.

"Settled!" said Timothy. And he looked at Priscilla with a great big-brother smile.

Priscilla smiled back at Timothy—and threw her sun hat on the floor.

The End

THE KIDS FROM APPLE STREET CHURCH

How did it happen?

Every day brings new excitement in the lives of Mary Jo, Danny, and the other kids from Apple Street Church. Whether it's finding a stolen doll in a coat sleeve, chasing important papers all over the school yard, meeting a famous astronaut, or discovering the real truth about a mysteriously broken leg, the kids write it all in their personal notebooks to God.

Usually diaries are private. But this is your chance to look over the shoulders of The Kids from Apple Street Church as they tell God about their secret thoughts, their problems, and their fun times. It's just like praying, except they are writing to God instead of talking to Him.

Don't miss any of the adventures of The Kids from Apple Street Church!

1. Mary Jo Bennett
2. Danny Petrowski
3. Julie Chang
4. Pug McConnell
5. Becky Garcia
6. Curtis Anderson

Available at your local Christian bookstore.

David C. Cook Publishing Co.
850 N. Grove Ave.
Elgin, IL 60120

Chariot Books

SHOELACES AND BRUSSELS SPROUTS

One little lie, but BIG trouble!

When Alex lies to her mom about losing her shoelaces, it doesn't seem like a big deal. But how do you replace special baseball laces when you don't have any money and you're not allowed to go to the store alone? A big softball game is coming up, and Alex knows the coach won't let her pitch in shoes without laces—or in cowboy boots!

Every kid gets into the predicaments that Alex does—ones that start out small and mushroom. Readers will learn from Alex's mistakes and understand that they have the same sources of help that she turns to: A God who loves them and wants to help them, and parents who understand.

Other books in the Alex Series . . .

2 *French Fry Forgiveness*—Sometimes making friends is harder than making enemies.

3 *Hot Chocolate Friendship*—Is winning first place as important to Alex as being a friend?

4 *Peanut Butter and Jelly Secrets*—Obeying her parents (even in little things) beats the awful results of disobeying.

Available at your local Christian bookstore.

David C. Cook Publishing Co.
850 N. Grove Ave.
Elgin, IL 60120

Chariot Books